# the
# Princess's

Text by
FEDERICA MAGRIN

# Survival Guide

Illustrations by
LAURA BRENLLA

WSkids
WHITE STAR KIDS

# CONTENTS

# ARE YOU READY?

Would you like to become a princess?

Well, if that's the case then you must know that having riches and beauty is not enough, you also need to learn how to SURVIVE AGAINST EVIL QUEENS AND WITCHES, befriend helpful people and creatures that can defend you and give you a hand if there is an emergency, and find **POTIONS** and **WEAPONS** that can be used against all kinds of enemies.

A manual like this one, with the advice of a fairy godmother who has been working with princesses of undoubted fame for years, is exactly what you need.

But first, LET ME INTRODUCE MYSELF: my name is **SPARKLY**, I love all things shiny and sparkling, and I'm full of bright ideas!

I was born a fairy in... well, QUITE A LONG TIME AGO, inside a white and pink bellflower, and I got my "godmother" certificate after a long period of training...

YOU WOULDN'T BELIEVE HOW MANY
PRINCESSES I'VE HELPED!

Maybe you're wondering why I've decided to collect my experiences in this manual: it's easy, I THOUGHT FUTURE PRINCESSES MIGHT NEED SOME HELP. So I collected stories of the most famous princesses from all around the world:

**POCAHONTAS** from the United States,

**BEAUTY** from France,

**THAKANE** from Africa,

**THE LITTLE MERMAID** from the bottom of the ocean,

and many others who have shown their courage and determination, taking on several adversities before reaching their long-awaited happy ending...

When I had finished, I realized that reading these stories would be useful, but not enough, so I decided to add a lot of information about talking mirrors, genie lamps, mysterious towers, evil witches... in other words, ANYTHING THAT MIGHT HELP YOU FULLY FIND YOUR WAY IN THE MAGICAL WORLD OF PRINCES AND PRINCESSES.

ARE YOU READY FOR THIS
FANTASTIC TRIP THEN?

Just follow the sparks
I've made with my magic
wand and **FOLLOW ME** in
this book to find out how
you can become a perfect
princess but also, and
above all, a WONDERFUL
MODERNLY-TRADITIONAL
PRINCESS!

# SNOW WHITE

As white as snow, with lips as red as blood and hair as dark as ebony.
THE LOOKS OF A REAL PRINCESS.

It would all be perfect if it weren't for a very vain **stepmother** appearing
on the scene and her very nosy **magic mirror** blabbing out that the fairest
girl in the kingdom is Snow White. As you can imagine, the queen doesn't
take this news well and banishes her stepdaughter. But there's more: she
unleashes a hunter after her, ordering him TO KILL HER and TAKE HER HEART.
Luckily, the man takes pity on her and lets her go. The worst seems over,
but how can a helpless princess manage to survive alone in the forest?
The only thing she can do is... WORK HARD! So she walks and walks, and
then bumps into a small house and the **seven dwarves** living there, who
decide to take her as their guest.

AND THEY LIVED HAPPILY EVER AFTER?
Not at all, because that chatty magic mirror we talked about before tells
the queen that Snow White is still alive and still very beautiful. Obviously,
the stepmother is disappointed and plots her revenge: she disguises herself
as an old lady, takes a **poisoned apple** with her and rushes to find the girl
who, without really thinking much about it, bites it and falls, LOOKING DEAD.

WHAT A TRAGEDY!
The dwarves put the princess in a crystal coffin in the woods, without
knowing that the **prince** who will not save her directly, but helps her come
back to life, is soon going to pass there. And like in all real fairy tales,
THE PRINCE AND PRINCESS FALL IN LOVE AT FIRST SIGHT!

## AN EVIL QUEEN AND THEN?

What happens to the bad guys after they've been NEUTRALIZED? Some of them suffer a really BAD FATE made of dreadful punishments, while others aren't treated as badly as you would expect.

This is the case for Snow White's evil queen, who is simply asked TO LEAVE THE CASTLE AND NOT LET HERSELF BE SEEN AGAIN.

Of course, this is not great for someone who is so used to living in the limelight, but it could have been worse. Moreover, the princess is so sweet and kind that she even visits her every now and then. But she takes her own food with her, JUST TO BE ON THE SAFE SIDE.

## ANATOMY OF A MAGIC MIRROR

**1-** It SPEAKS and SPEAKS and SPEAKS. Even rambling sometimes.

**2-** It often reveals precious secrets and PUTS PEOPLE IN DANGER.

**3-** It prefers young princesses to evil queens.

**4-** It often CHANGES ITS SURFACE and lets you see things that aren't there.

**5-** It ALWAYS tells the truth, even when lying would be better.

Therefore...
NEVER TRUST A MAGIC MIRROR!

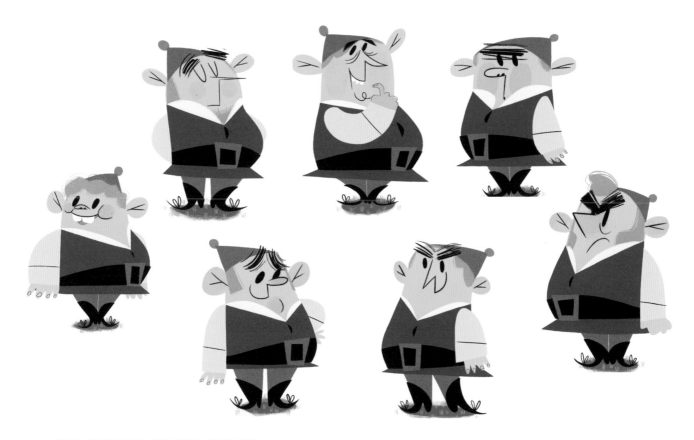

## THE MORAL OF THE STORY

SOMETIMES BEING VERY BEAUTIFUL IS NOT SO GREAT, especially when you're dealing with evil queens. There are never enough helpers. If you end up with 7, like Snow White, you should be quite safe, if old ladies allow it.

If they offer you something, even something that looks like a harmless apple, say "Thank you!" but always firmly decline. HUNTERS ARE NOT ALWAYS BAD, ESPECIALLY THOSE WHO ARE ASKED TO KILL UNLUCKY PRINCESSES.

## A KISS? NO, IT WASN'T!

Many think that Snow White was saved by the prince's kiss. BUT IT'S NOT TRUE AT ALL! What brought her back to life was actually an accident. What really happened could appear on a COMEDY SHOW: when pulling up the crystal coffin where the princess was lying, the prince's servants tripped, making the poor princess tumble down. The piece of poisoned apple fell out of her mouth and Snow White started breathing again.

This means that sometimes YOU NEED A LITTLE BIT OF LUCK TO SURVIVE IN FAIRY TALES.

# THE LITTLE MERMAID

Being happy with what we have is sometimes difficult, even for a **princess**!

There are those with raven-black hair that dream about being blond, or those who expect a prince and end up with a frog. There are also those who live in a beautiful **underwater castle**, like the daughter of the **King of the Ocean**, and wish for nothing but a trip on land! This is why her 15TH-BIRTHDAY gift is the best one ever: she's finally able to surface from the ocean's depths.

Her to-see list is full of lawns, castles and hills but, as soon as the young mermaid pops up between the waves, all she sees is the ROYAL VESSEL where the birthday festivities for a charming dark-eyed **prince** with a kind smile are taking place. The **little mermaid** doesn't need to think twice: THE DAY'S PROGRAM IS SET ASIDE!

Well, that's also because, in the meantime, a storm has made the boat sink and THERE'S A PRINCE TO SAVE! When she's back underwater, she takes a drastic decision: she'll go to the **sea witch** and ask her to make her HUMAN. However, you must remember that ALL MAGICAL ACTS HAVE A PRICE...

The little mermaid must GIVE HER VOICE TO THE WITCH, and she'll lose her life if the prince marries another girl. And this is what actually happens, as **Ariel**, who is as voiceless as we are speechless when we hear about this sad ending, is not able to make herself be recognized by the prince.

She's forced to honor her pact with the witch and makes do with becoming an immortal "DAUGHTER OF THE AIR."

## UNDER THE SEA

The world of princesses is made of CASTLES with very high towers; sea princesses like the little mermaid also live in similar places, BUT THERE ARE SOME INEVITABLE DIFFERENCES:

**1-** Plants and trees surround the castle, but the water makes them move all the time, forming CORRIDORS WITH EVER-CHANGING DESIGNS.

**2-** The royal carriage doesn't have wheels and it's PULLED BY SEA ANIMALS (DOLPHINS mostly).

**3-** Instead of twirling birds there are MULTI-COLORED FISH SWIMMING AROUND.

## ANATOMY OF A MERMAID

SHE DOESN'T HAVE LEGS but a wonderful, colorful tail like a fish. She doesn't wear jewelry or lavish clothes, BUT ADORNS HERSELF WITH SHELLS, CORALS AND SEA FLOWERS.
Her melodic singing can CHARM THE SAILORS THAT PASS BY, but if she loses her voice because she has a cold or has been cursed, her life gets much more complicated!

## A GRANDMOTHER'S ADVICE

Grandmothers are famous for their apple pies, their uncommon wisdom, for being able to cheer up their granddaughters and FOR GIVING ADVICE ABOUT EVERYTHING: SCHOOL, FRIENDS, FASHION AND LOVE. The little mermaid's grandmother gives truly exceptional advice. She's the one, for example, who tells her granddaughter to wear eight big oysters on her tail to go to the surface. And when the little mermaid complains about THE SHELLS HURTING HER, the grandmother says the words every princess hears at some point in her life: "NO PAIN, NO GAIN!"

## IN THE CAVE OF A SEA WITCH

Witches, as you know, love living in the GLOOMIEST, most desolate PLACES, but the sea witch outdoes them all. In order to get there, you must go through a seething marsh and face CREATURES THAT ARE PART PLANTS AND PART ANIMALS, their TENTACLES stretching out to catch whoever dares to pass there.

# BADROULBADOUR

**Badroulbadour**, full moon of full moons.
With a name like this, princess Badroulbadour could never be less than charming.
It is not strange, therefore, for **Aladdin** to fall in love with her at first sight when
he sees her walking around the street.

The boy, who became rich thanks to the **genie in the lamp**, which he found in a DESERT
CAVE, stealing it from a powerful sorcerer, is charmed by the girl's captivating gaze
and decides to ask her hand in MARRIAGE.

THINGS ARE COMPLICATED AT FIRST. Badroulbadour is, in fact, engaged to be married
to the **son** of the **great vizier**, who is also a strong **wizard**.
Aladdin, however, is not one who gets discouraged easily and, on the other hand,
Badroulbadour knows what she wants. In the end, the two manage to convince the **sultan**
to fulfill their dreams, BUT THE MARRIAGE IS NOT AN EASY ONE.

After all, as you know, this is always the case when dealing with merciless wizards!
Badroulbadour is, in fact, kidnapped by the evil necromancer, who wants to put his hands
on the **magic lamp**. Aladdin immediately tries to find her, but the princess manages
to save herself in the end.

HOW? By persuading the wizard to drink a cup of
wine laced with a STRONG SLEEPING DRAUGHT.
Once he's asleep, ALADDIN CAN EASILY BEAT
HIM and live happily ever after with his
beloved Badroulbadour.

## A FRIENDLY GENIE

What you have always known as a GENIE is actually a JINN, a creature that can be friendly and nice or cruel and vindictive. Before getting in contact with a genie then, it is better to make sure he's one of the good kind.
HOW CAN YOU TELL? Easy, just follow these steps:

1- MAKE A WISH. If he grants it, he has accepted you as its master, otherwise... RUN!

2- If only good things happen to you after meeting him, then you've met a genie that brings good luck. DON'T LET IT RUN AWAY!

3- If, after rubbing a magic lamp, no genie comes out, it may be a GROUCHY one: he'll help you in the end, but always reluctantly. In this case, PROMISE YOU'LL MAKE HIM FREE; the effects on his spirits will be incredible!

## ANATOMY OF A MAGIC LAMP

It has a chubby shape, to accommodate the genie, a lid on top, to keep it inside, and a long spout, to let it out when you want its help. If it's been hidden in a magic cave for centuries, it might be a bit DUSTY, but be careful when you clean it: A STRONGER RUB AND THE GENIE WILL WAKE UP! It can also come in handy if you need to light a room, but it's better to use it to have wishes granted.

## A FAIRY TALE PALACE

Try to imagine the biggest and most LAVISH PALACE you have ever seen.
Well, I can assure you that is nothing compared to princess Badroulbadour's.
Imagine this, there is an enormous ballroom that could fit hundreds of people,
with 24 windows framed by precious gems.
I don't want to bore you with all those extraordinary bedrooms,
multi-equipped bathrooms and wonderful gardens, but I must tell
you a secret: THERE IS A TREASURE ROOM HIDDEN IN THE PALACE,
WHICH NO ONE HAS EVER SEEN.

## NOT ONLY WITCHES, BUT ALSO WIZARDS!

I've warned you several times about cruel, vindictive
witches, those who often prevent princesses from
fulfilling their dreams. Well, I don't want to
discourage you, but there are also WIZARDS
that are as tough and without scruples!
In order to get a magic lamp, the evil wizard
Aladdin met travelled around the world and didn't
have second thoughts when it came to cheating,
stealing, and kidnapping.
SOMETHING THAT WOULD SHAME EVEN THE MOST
RUTHLESS WITCH!

# BEAUTY

Her name is **Beauty**, her strength however doesn't lie in her charms but in her ability to LOOK BEYOND APPEARANCES, even when they are **monstrous**!
She's an incurable optimist: she even manages to find a silver lining when her father loses all his wealth, even though things actually go worse and worse...

Few characters in Fairy tale Land have been as unlucky as **Beauty's father**, actually! When coming back from a trip that should have restored his wealth but had actually left him hopeless, the poor man is caught up in a snowstorm, even though it's the middle of summer. He seeks shelter in a **castle** and, while he picks up a **rose** he would like to bring back to his daughter, he is attacked by the master of the house: a HORRIBLE, GIGANTIC, AND VERY ENRAGED CREATURE!
The **Beast** lets him go back home, but this isn't a good thing at all: BEAUTY MUST TAKE HIS PLACE. The girl obviously offers to go to the castle to protect her father, and this is actually something good, because she's the only one who can see what really lies under all that fur, in the master of the house's heart.

The Beast falls in love with Beauty in just a few seconds; well, what monster could ever resist a girl who's NOT AFRAID TO DANCE WITH HIM, despite his big, ugly paws? So, he allows her to go back home to take care of her sick father (I told you, this man's really unlucky). Her envious and malicious sisters, however, make her stay for a long time, and BEAUTY COMES BACK LATE TO THE CASTLE, when the Beast is so hurt and sick he's almost dead.

Desperate, Beauty leans down to **kiss him** and her true love's kiss not only saves him, it also BREAKS THE CURSE and turns him back into the handsome prince he used to be.

## A BEASTLY PRINCE

If the princes you have in mind are always young handsome men, that are strong, with a noble spirit and richly dressed, who wear a shining armor and ride a strong horse, then well, YOU COULD BE VERY SURPRISED! There are actually many different kinds of princes: there are those who look like MONSTERS or those who appear in the form of frogs or mice. Often, all they need to turn back into real, textbook princes is the kiss of a princess or of a girl with a big heart.

BE CAREFUL THOUGH: not all the mice and frogs you bump into are princes, so try to find out more about them before using one of YOUR KISSES!

## ANATOMY OF AN ENCHANTED CASTLE

It looks like any other princely manor, but it's surrounded by a mysterious aura and sometimes even has an ENCHANTED GARDEN. It's often enveloped by a timeless fog or hidden in a forest populated by CREATURES that have strange powers. IT'S HOME TO CREATURES THAT LOOK LIKE MONSTERS BUT SOMETIMES HAVE ONLY BEEN CURSED.

## POISONOUS RELATIONS

In a fairy tale you must always
watch out for any possible envious
relative who might prevent you
from reaching that long awaited
happy ending.
Take BEAUTY for example: she
risked not coming back to the castle
in time, almost didn't have her happy
ending...
AND IT WAS ALL HER SISTERS' FAULT!
In order to tell if there are hidden enemies in
your family, you need to pay close attention
to their behavior:

**1-** They would like to convince you to go
on a journey in a very far land and are
particularly pushy when you refuse to leave.

**2-** They ask to borrow your clothes, make-up and
jewels, and when you ask them back, they lie and
pretend that stuff has always been theirs.

**3-** They distract you and make you
arrive late for very important
appointments.

# BRIAR ROSE

Like many other princesses, when **Briar Rose** is born everyone is
surprised by her BEAUTY AND SWEET NATURE. The whole kingdom,
charmed by the little one, is already expecting a happy ending, but one
can never take things for granted in FAIRY TALES: even the smallest
distraction can have catastrophic consequences!

While busy organizing a royal christening, the **king** and **queen** forget to
send their invitation to a strong and rather crabby **witch**.
During the festivities, while some **good fairies** are giving gifts to the baby
(kindness, cheerfulness, goodness... well, they always ask us fairies for the
same presents), the witch bursts into the scene to cast a **terrible curse**
on the child: when she grows up, SHE WILL PRICK HER FINGER ON THE
SPINDLE OF A SPINNING WHEEL AND DIE!

Luckily, the youngest **fairy godmother** manages to change the curse so
that, instead of dying, Briar Rose would FALL ASLEEP FOR ONE HUNDRED
YEARS. It's unfortunate that she couldn't also grant the baby her gift, a
little wisdom. It would have come in handy as, in fact, eighteen years later
the princess manages to find the only spinning wheel left in the kingdom,
prickle her finger on its spindle, and **fall asleep**.

MANY THINGS CAN HAPPEN IN A CENTURY, some neglected thorny bushes,
for example, can grow so much in the royal garden they even end up
covering the whole castle!

Now it's time for a **prince** to save the day. He doesn't have a green
thumb but a SHINING SWORD he confidently uses to make his way
through that jungle of branches and roots, until he reaches Briar Rose
who wakes up, rested and smiling, thanks to his **light kiss**.

## A PRINCE IN THREE STEPS

There are princesses that save themselves, some who save their better half, and those who need a LITTLE HELP. Take poor Briar Rose for example: asleep, locked up in the tower of a castle and, if that wasn't enough, surrounded by thorns so thick even the light couldn't get through. What could she do without a helping hand? So, in these cases, the only solution is having a fairy tale prince come timely into action.

BUT WHY HIM?

**1-** He's stubborn: if there's a princess in danger, nothing can stop him, even if he's a hundred years late;

**2-** He always has a sharp sword with him: perfect for cutting infesting weeds.

**3-** He's super fit, enough to climb up the over one thousand steps leading to the top of the castle's highest tower.

## GOOD AND BAD FAIRIES

There are fairies and fairies...
I, for example, am good, even though I have
some flaws, but I know some that, believe
me, you're better off without them.
The bad one in Briar Rose's story is ONE
OF THE WORST. Not only does she have a bad temper,
she's also capable of devising a very complex plan to
take a long-term revenge on a tiny, helpless princess.

## GOOD NIGHT!

Sleeping is good for you. This is surely true for Briar Rose, who looked very rested
when she woke up. No wonder she's called "SLEEPING BEAUTY."

SO MY ADVICE IS TO NOT BE AFRAID OF BOREDOM OR A LACK OF ACTION: RESTING
WILL HELP YOU STAY FOCUSED AND CALM AT ALL TIMES, EVEN BEFORE MEETING YOUR
PRINCE CHARMING.

## ANATOMY OF A SPINNING WHEEL

If you're wondering what a SPINNING WHEEL is,
well it's an old tool people used to spin with.
The most dangerous part, especially if you are
in a fairy tale, is the SPINDLE, because it can
prick you and put terrible curses into action.
It's extremely difficult to find one nowadays,
but even a modern princess must be careful
and avoid cursed objects, as they're not always
forgotten in the secret chamber of a castle's
most distant tower.

# CINDERELLA

NICKNAMES! Princesses fear them as much as everyone else! Some are good-natured —
admittedly, being remembered as "sleeping beauty" is not the worst thing that can happen
to you — but other ones are a true curse! Take **Cinderella** for example: as if being forced
by your **stepmother** to clean your whole house and SLEEPING IN THE ASHES next to the
fireplace wasn't enough, this kind girl with a golden heart must also endure her **stepsisters**,
who give her one of those nicknames it's impossible to get rid of!
She gets her chance when the household receives an **invitation to a ball** the sovereign
is organizing so that his son may FIND A GIRL TO MARRY.

The stepmother prevents Cinderella from participating, but somebody finally comes
to help her: a **fairy godmother** who turns that dusty, desperate girl into a royal-looking
princess, ready to get to the ball on a lavish **carriage**, wearing an unforgettable dress
and two uncomfortable but lovely **glass slippers**.
There's only one restriction: she must leave the palace **before midnight**, when the spell
will vanish. **Time**, however, runs fast when you have fun, and Cinderella notices the bell
is tolling only at the last second: she must run away, **losing a slipper**
in the meantime.

The **prince** immediately starts looking for the
girl he fell in love with, deciding to have ALL
GIRLS IN THE KINGDOM TRY THE SHOE ON.
When it's finally the young girl's turn, the
precious shoe perfectly fits her tiny foot!
Cinderella can now MARRY HER PRINCE
and live happily, although not even her
fairy godmother can get rid of the
girl's famous nickname.

## ANATOMY OF A FAIRY GODMOTHER

I don't want to brag, but not all fairies can call themselves
"GODMOTHER": it's a very particular kind of qualification that
requires years of studying and some special qualities.
HERE ARE THE MAIN ONES:

**1-** IMAGINATION
Cinderella's fairy godmother has
plenty of it, as she's able to throw
something together with what
she finds in the vegetable patch,
transforming a pumpkin and two
mice into a LAVISH CARRIAGE pulled
by two elegant white horses.

**2-** GOOD TIMING
We need to get to our
unlucky heroine at the
RIGHT TIME. If she had
been even one day late,
Cinderella would have
missed the ball!

**3-** GOOD TASTE
A keen eye for fashion
is essential when
turning dirty rugs into
a royal gown. And those
glass slippers? Wow!
UNFORGETTABLE!

## WARNINGS FOR AN UNEVENTFUL BALL

If you are invited to a royal ball there are some things to carefully take into
consideration if you want TO AVOID HAVING PROBLEMS:

**1-** Bring a watch with you,
so that you can calmly and
elegantly exit the scene
before midnight.

**2-** Put a mask on to
avoid being recognized
by your stepmother,
if she's there.

**3-** Don't introduce
yourself to the king by
the ridiculous nickname
your stepsisters gave you.

## VERY SPECIAL LITTLE SHOES

They're stiff, could make you slip
on the castle's steps and slid off
your feet as you start running away.
Nevertheless, GLASS SLIPPERS are
always into fashion for balls, as they
have an undeniable ADVANTAGE: they
are custom made and no other girl in
the kingdom, except for you, will ever
be able to wear the same pair.

## POISONOUS RELATIVES

There are several princesses who
grew up with not-so-loving parents
or guardians. Take SNOW WHITE,
for example, who lives with a ruthless
witch. Or RAPUNZEL, forced to
boringly live within the walls of
a tiny tower for years.
And yet, CINDERELLA'S STEPMOTHER
AND STEPSISTERS would definitely win
the prize for "worse relatives in Fairy
tale Land." And they're SO CRUEL
they're proud of it!

# DONKEYSKIN

There is someone who became famous for her
skin as white as snow and someone for her...
**Donkeyskin**!
And yet I can guarantee that the latter was born as
a "VERY NORMAL" PRINCESS in a kingdom governed
by kind sovereigns. When the queen dies though,
an ambitious **councilor** convinces the **king** to let his
daughter become his bride, without her consent.

The princess tries everything she can TO AVOID GETTING MARRIED! First of all,
the wedding gift she asks her father are **three dresses** that not even us fairies would
be able to make. Unfortunately, the court seamstress is a true artist and the dresses
she sews are exactly what the princess asked for.
The princess is dramatically short of ideas so she tries playing her last, desperate
card and asks for a **cloak made of donkey skin**: it's the most important animal
in the whole kingdom!

When this wish is also unexpectedly granted, the young maiden decides to RUN AWAY
FROM THE CASTLE, hidden under the donkey skin. Without a destination, she wanders
for days until she reaches a farm where, as she looks so bizarre, SHE'S GIVEN THE
TASK OF LOOKING AFTER THE ANIMALS. Every now and then though, when there is
a holiday, the princess takes out one of the three royal dresses she has brought
with her and, after having a long bath, she puts them on to feel less sad.
It's on one of these days that a wandering **prince** sees her through the keyhole
and falls in love with her.

When he's back at the palace, the prince thinks so much about that girl he falls sick,
but he finds out that there is a bizarre girl who looks after the pigs living in that
tiny hut. This doesn't stop him: he insists so much that DONKEYSKIN IS CALLED TO THE
COURT. The princess thus finally takes her donkey skin off, revealing her true identity,
and fulfills her dreams by marrying the prince.

**MY HEART,
MY CHOICE!**

This is what Donkeyskin must have thought when she found out they had arranged her marriage BEHIND HER BACK, without asking for her consent, of course. She's so OUTRAGED she's rather give up everything to keep her freedom!

**YOU CAN'T TELL
A PRINCESS BY
HER DRESS**

Admit it, when you think of a princess, you imagine a beautiful girl wearing long, elegant gowns, a crown on her head and not a hair out of place. Many of them were and still are like this, but this kind of princess, believe me, is QUITE OVERRATED. What's more in fashion is... putting fashion aside to get the looks that better fit our PERSONALITY and TASTES.

## BAD ADVICE FROM BAD ADVISORS

The true baddy in this fairy tale doesn't have magic powers, his ability to manipulate others with his MELLIFLUOUS WORDS is enough. I'm speaking about the king's evil advisor, the one who convinces the king to sacrifice his daughter's happiness to inherit the throne. Beware of people like him and DEFEND YOURSELF by always using your head to tell what's right and wrong!

## ANATOMY OF AN UNCONVENTIONAL COUPLE

Both main characters in this story are quite ODD. Donkeyskin, as we know, is a princess who decides to leave her castle to go living on a FARM but, when you think about it, the prince is an aristocrat who would marry a PIG HERDER without hesitation.

He's not bothered by his beloved alleged low birth and his perseverance is rewarded with Donkeyskin's love.

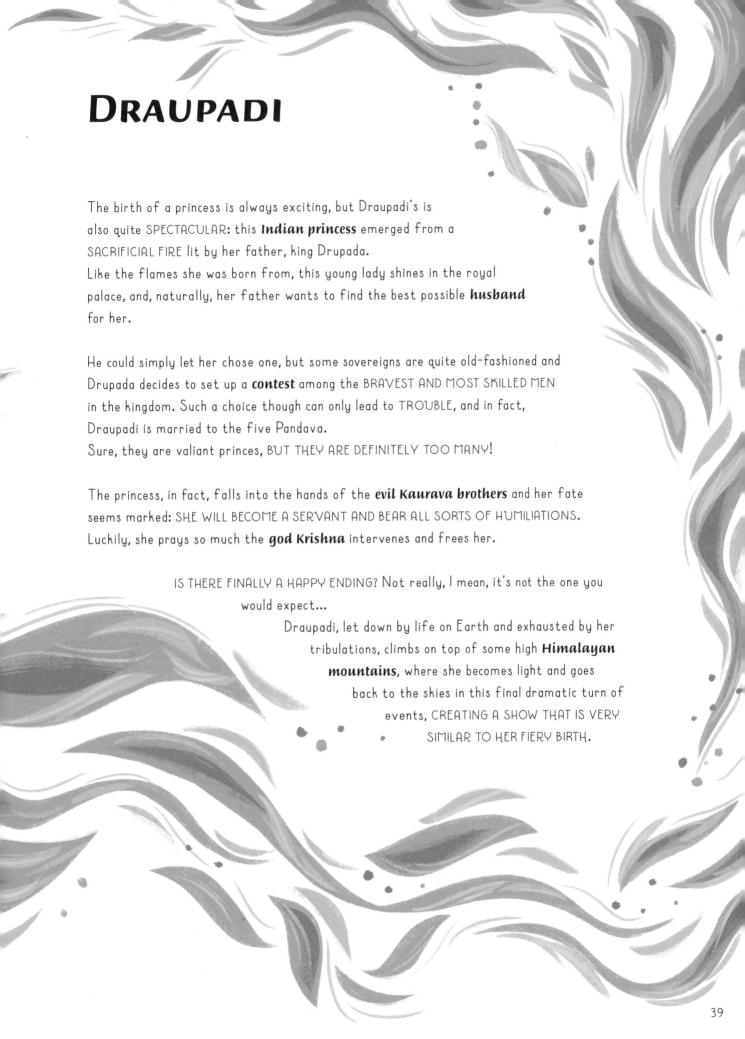

# DRAUPADI

The birth of a princess is always exciting, but Draupadi's is also quite SPECTACULAR: this **Indian princess** emerged from a SACRIFICIAL FIRE lit by her father, king Drupada.
Like the flames she was born from, this young lady shines in the royal palace, and, naturally, her father wants to find the best possible **husband** for her.

He could simply let her chose one, but some sovereigns are quite old-fashioned and Drupada decides to set up a **contest** among the BRAVEST AND MOST SKILLED MEN in the kingdom. Such a choice though can only lead to TROUBLE, and in fact, Draupadi is married to the five Pandava.
Sure, they are valiant princes, BUT THEY ARE DEFINITELY TOO MANY!

The princess, in fact, falls into the hands of the **evil Kaurava brothers** and her fate seems marked: SHE WILL BECOME A SERVANT AND BEAR ALL SORTS OF HUMILIATIONS.
Luckily, she prays so much the **god Krishna** intervenes and frees her.

IS THERE FINALLY A HAPPY ENDING? Not really, I mean, it's not the one you would expect...
Draupadi, let down by life on Earth and exhausted by her tribulations, climbs on top of some high **Himalayan mountains**, where she becomes light and goes back to the skies in this final dramatic turn of events, CREATING A SHOW THAT IS VERY SIMILAR TO HER FIERY BIRTH.

## THERE ISN'T ALWAYS A HAPPY ENDING

There aren't many unlucky princesses, that's true, but
I still need to warn you: happy endings aren't always certain.
Both DRAUPADI and the LITTLE MERMAID know this well: everything
can go wrong at any time and a royal title is no guarantee for
a "happily ever after."
Sure, luck can give us some help but, to be on the safe side,
IT'S BETTER TO DO ALL WE CAN TO FIND HAPPINESS!

## ANATOMY OF AN INDIAN PRINCESS

Princesses coming from India are unmistakable. They don't wear
poofy dresses, crowns on their heads or shoes on their feet.
Their look is very original and includes:
a **SARI**: this is a drape that is wrapped around the waist with one
end draped around the shoulder so that it gently falls on the
back. It seems very simple, but it's actually difficult to wear
and has a very old tradition;
the **CHOLI**, a finely decorated blouse that leaves the midriff
bare and must be worn under the sari;
**SANDALS**, but not the ones you wear to go to the beach in
summer! They must be studded with stones that shine in the sun.

A LOT OF JEWELS!
The most used are the **NATH**, a nose ring,
the **MAANG TIKKA**, which decorates
the hair parting, the **ARSI**, a ring to
wear on the thumb, and the **KARN
PHOOL**, which means "flowers on
your ears" and are earrings which
cover the whole ear.

## A GODLY FRIEND

Fairy godmothers like me are usually the ones who help princesses in distress, but don't forget that other magical, supernatural beings or even gods could feel sorry for a maiden in the middle of a crisis! Draupadi hersef is helped by no less than KRISHNA, the earthly version of god VISNU.

## THIRD EYE

When facing apparently impossible challenges, sometimes TWO EYES ARE NOT ENOUGH, this is why Draupadi uses a third one! This is called **AJNA**, it's invisible and it's more or less between the eyes. BUT WHAT IS IT FOR? We use it to develop our IMAGINATION and CREATIVITY, to find solutions where we tend to see obstacles and problems. These are fundamental features for a princess, so you should really start to train!

YOU DON'T NEED MAGIC TO MAKE IT APPEAR THOUGH, BUT A HUGE AMOUNT OF MEDITATION.

# FROG PRINCESS

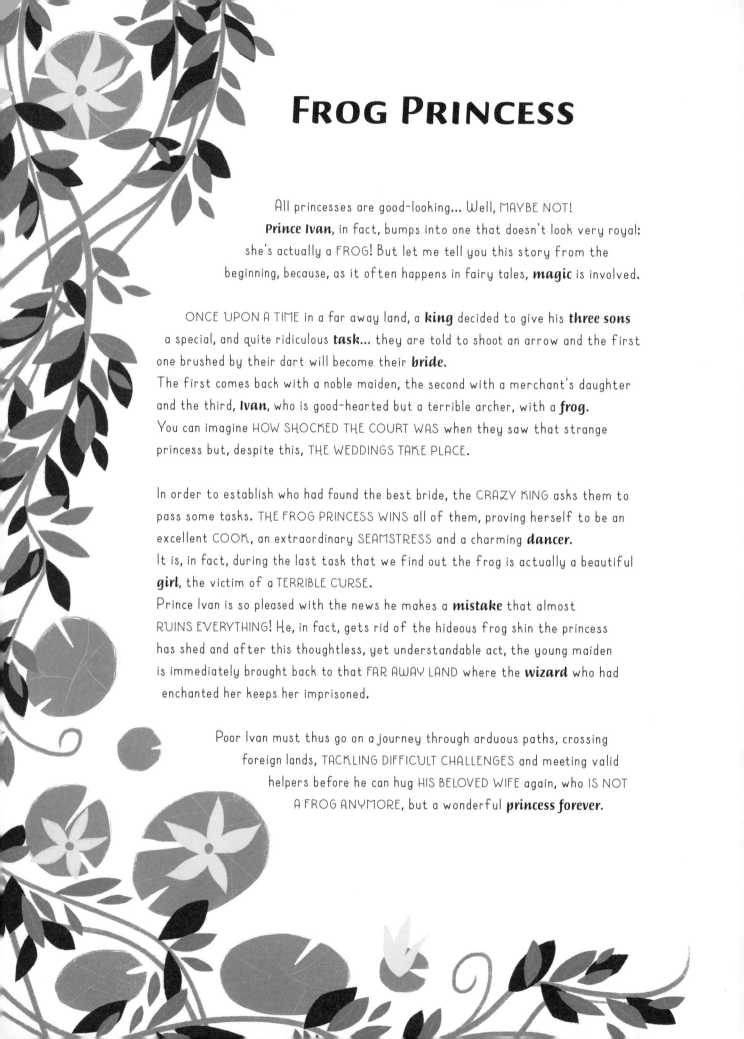

All princesses are good-looking... Well, MAYBE NOT!
**Prince Ivan**, in fact, bumps into one that doesn't look very royal:
she's actually a FROG! But let me tell you this story from the
beginning, because, as it often happens in fairy tales, **magic** is involved.

ONCE UPON A TIME in a far away land, a **king** decided to give his **three sons**
a special, and quite ridiculous **task**... they are told to shoot an arrow and the first
one brushed by their dart will become their **bride**.
The first comes back with a noble maiden, the second with a merchant's daughter
and the third, **Ivan**, who is good-hearted but a terrible archer, with a **frog**.
You can imagine HOW SHOCKED THE COURT WAS when they saw that strange
princess but, despite this, THE WEDDINGS TAKE PLACE.

In order to establish who had found the best bride, the CRAZY KING asks them to
pass some tasks. THE FROG PRINCESS WINS all of them, proving herself to be an
excellent COOK, an extraordinary SEAMSTRESS and a charming **dancer**.
It is, in fact, during the last task that we find out the frog is actually a beautiful
**girl**, the victim of a TERRIBLE CURSE.
Prince Ivan is so pleased with the news he makes a **mistake** that almost
RUINS EVERYTHING! He, in fact, gets rid of the hideous frog skin the princess
has shed and after this thoughtless, yet understandable act, the young maiden
is immediately brought back to that FAR AWAY LAND where the **wizard** who had
enchanted her keeps her imprisoned.

Poor Ivan must thus go on a journey through arduous paths, crossing
foreign lands, TACKLING DIFFICULT CHALLENGES and meeting valid
helpers before he can hug HIS BELOVED WIFE again, who IS NOT
A FROG ANYMORE, but a wonderful **princess forever**.

## ... AND FROG PRINCE

If there are frog princesses, well, you should know there are also FROG PRINCES!
A princess who is both beautiful and fussy bumps into one of these.
Well, we can't really blame her: few girls would want to hug, let alone kiss,
a SLIMY GREEN-BROWN TOAD FULL OF LUMPS!
But remember that a person with a HEART OF GOLD can be hidden behind very
UNATTRACTIVE LOOKS.

## THE COURTSHIPS
## OF CLUMSY PRINCES!

Young Ivan wins his bride over in a very
particular way: HE POKES HER WITH AN
ARROW BY MISTAKE. Not all princes ride a
white horse and appear in all their splendor
and braveness.
Some of them trip over things, have a
terrible aim or are shy and clumsy.

## THE TRIALS
## OF THE PERFECT BRIDE

The king of this fairy tale keeps coming
up with increasingly BIZARRE IDEAS.
First that wheeze about how to
choose a wife for his sons, then those
competitions that, between you and me,
are all quite banal: MUSIC, SEWING and
DANCING.
Hmm, shall we propose some more
interesting challenges?

WHAT ARE YOU GOOD AT?
I'M A WHIZ AT POTIONS, FLYING SCIENCE
AND WAND ACROBATICS.

# KAGUYA-HIME

Also known as the SHINING PRINCESS, **Kaguya-hime** is found
by chance in a very unexpected place: INSIDE THE STALK OF A
BAMBOO PLANT. The bamboo cutter who finds her brings her
home to his wife and they raise the girl as if she were their
**daughter**, even though she's tiny (SMALLER THAN A THUMB!).

The fact that she's an exceptional, maybe even MAGICAL, being
becomes apparent when the man, after welcoming her into his home,
starts finding **gold nuggets** in the bamboos he picks up.

Once she's grown up, Kaguya-hime becomes so BEAUTIFUL that many men
come from all around the kingdom because they wish to MARRY HER.
The girl asks all **princes** who ask her hand in marriage to pass such **difficult
tasks** that NO ONE IS BRAVE ENOUGH TO RISK TRYING.

Even the **emperor** doesn't manage to win over the girl's heart, and this is not
because she thinks herself superior to him, but because she knows SHE DOESN'T
BELONG TO EARTH. In fact, ONE SUMMER NIGHT, while gazing at the **Moon**, she
understands that she must go back there, where she was born, and sure enough,
a few days later some **celestial creatures** descend on Earth to take her home.

The emperor doesn't want to lose her (after all, WHO WOULD LET
AN ALIEN PRINCESS GO AWAY!) and sends an **entire army** to
stop her. However, the BEINGS coming from the **City of the
Moon** stop the soldiers with their **light** and manage to let
the Shining Princess go back to the SKY.

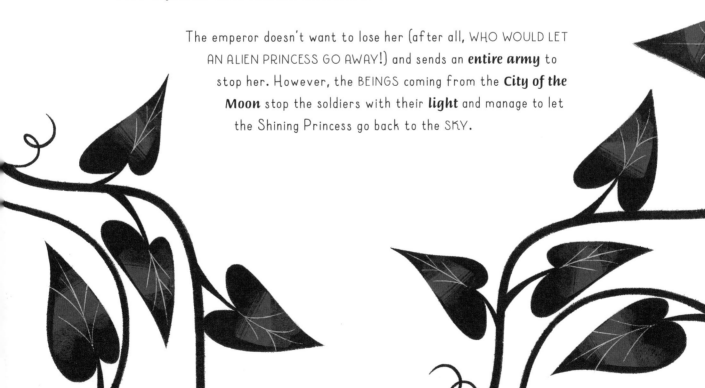

## ANATOMY OF AN ALIEN PRINCESS

SHE COMES FROM ANOTHER WORLD, but not necessarily from outer space. Whether it's the Moon, Mars or a wandering comet, what's sure is that her house is definitely not like yours!

**1-** She usually has SPECIAL POWERS, she can read people's minds, emanate light, change her shape or make objects, even very valuable ones, appear out of the blue.

**2-** She tends to get sad when she gets homesick but if you keep her busy by having TEA PARTIES with friends or a sleepover, she can be a VERY FUNNY PLAYMATE.

## A DRESS MADE TO FLY

I can't really say what are the perfect clothes for a princess, as they all wear incredibly different dresses, hairstyles and accessories. I mean: there are some who wear GLASS SLIPPERS that look really delicate, and others who don't even have feet but a MULTI-COLORED FISH-LIKE TAIL!
The dress worn by the SHINING PRINCESS, for example, is truly unmatchable: it's all covered in feathers and allows her TO FLY. When she goes back to the Moon, therefore, she doesn't need a spaceship or an alien flying saucer: she just puts her dress on and she can fly out like a ROCKET.

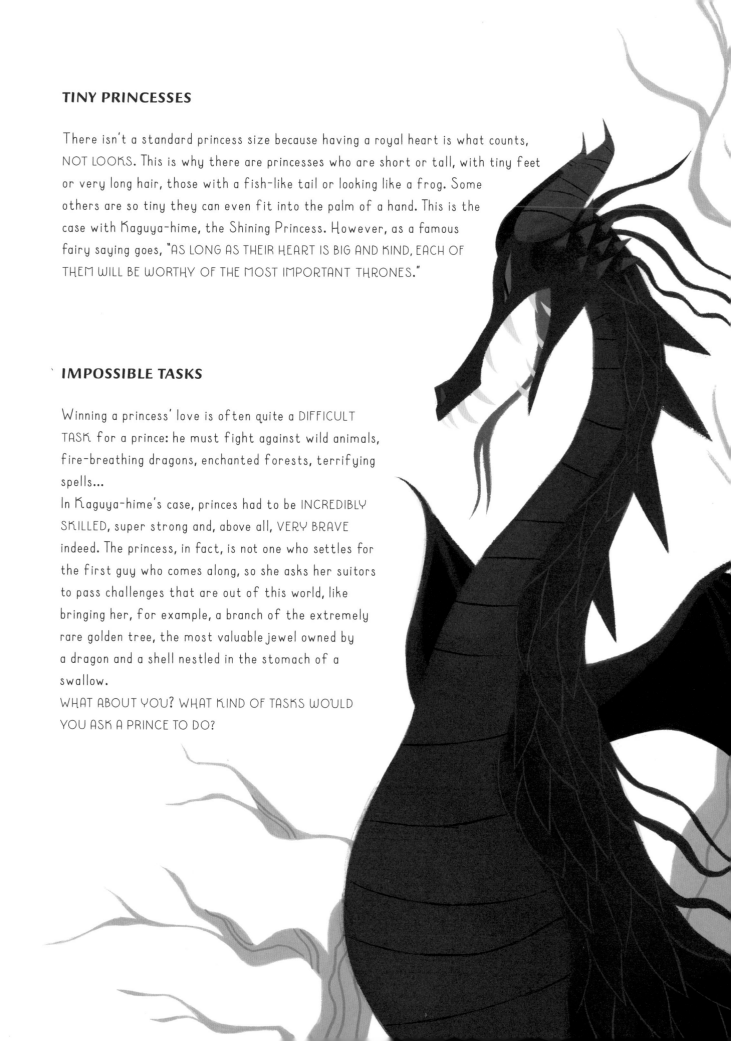

## TINY PRINCESSES

There isn't a standard princess size because having a royal heart is what counts, NOT LOOKS. This is why there are princesses who are short or tall, with tiny feet or very long hair, those with a fish-like tail or looking like a frog. Some others are so tiny they can even fit into the palm of a hand. This is the case with Kaguya-hime, the Shining Princess. However, as a famous fairy saying goes, "AS LONG AS THEIR HEART IS BIG AND KIND, EACH OF THEM WILL BE WORTHY OF THE MOST IMPORTANT THRONES."

## IMPOSSIBLE TASKS

Winning a princess' love is often quite a DIFFICULT TASK for a prince: he must fight against wild animals, fire-breathing dragons, enchanted forests, terrifying spells...
In Kaguya-hime's case, princes had to be INCREDIBLY SKILLED, super strong and, above all, VERY BRAVE indeed. The princess, in fact, is not one who settles for the first guy who comes along, so she asks her suitors to pass challenges that are out of this world, like bringing her, for example, a branch of the extremely rare golden tree, the most valuable jewel owned by a dragon and a shell nestled in the stomach of a swallow.
WHAT ABOUT YOU? WHAT KIND OF TASKS WOULD YOU ASK A PRINCE TO DO?

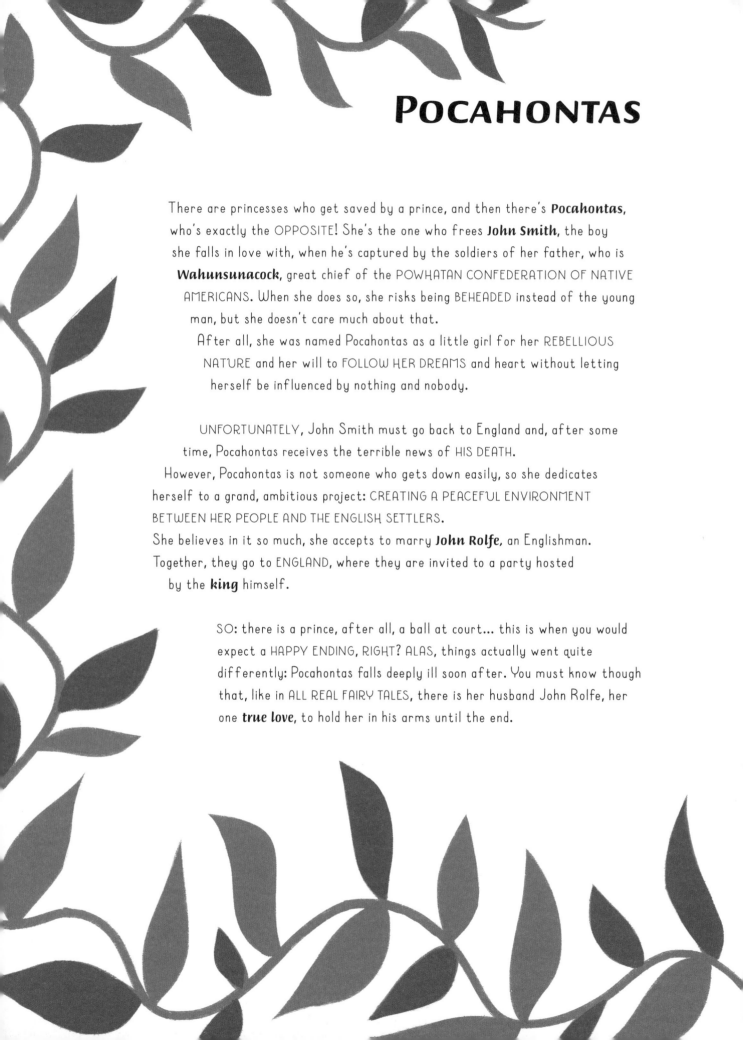

# POCAHONTAS

There are princesses who get saved by a prince, and then there's **Pocahontas**, who's exactly the OPPOSITE! She's the one who frees **John Smith**, the boy she falls in love with, when he's captured by the soldiers of her father, who is **Wahunsunacock**, great chief of the POWHATAN CONFEDERATION OF NATIVE AMERICANS. When she does so, she risks being BEHEADED instead of the young man, but she doesn't care much about that.

After all, she was named Pocahontas as a little girl for her REBELLIOUS NATURE and her will to FOLLOW HER DREAMS and heart without letting herself be influenced by nothing and nobody.

UNFORTUNATELY, John Smith must go back to England and, after some time, Pocahontas receives the terrible news of HIS DEATH.

However, Pocahontas is not someone who gets down easily, so she dedicates herself to a grand, ambitious project: CREATING A PEACEFUL ENVIRONMENT BETWEEN HER PEOPLE AND THE ENGLISH SETTLERS.

She believes in it so much, she accepts to marry **John Rolfe**, an Englishman. Together, they go to ENGLAND, where they are invited to a party hosted by the **king** himself.

SO: there is a prince, after all, a ball at court... this is when you would expect a HAPPY ENDING, RIGHT? ALAS, things actually went quite differently: Pocahontas falls deeply ill soon after. You must know though that, like in ALL REAL FAIRY TALES, there is her husband John Rolfe, her one **true love**, to hold her in his arms until the end.

## ANATOMY OF A NATIVE PRINCESS

There are princesses who are more suitable to fairy tale castles, those who live underwater, and finally, those who spend their life surrounded by the WILDEST NATURE ON EARTH. You can easily recognize them because:

**1-** They don't wear lavish CLOTHES, but only tops made of LEAVES, leather skirts and shirts, necklaces made of SHELLS or STONES.

**2-** They don't spruce up THEIR HAIR with crowns or precious hairpins, instead, they wear it down on their shoulders or, at most, tie it in a simple braid.

**3-** They love their FREEDOM, and not being forced to have long conversations or exhausting balls.

**POCAHONTAS: TRUE AND FALSE**

Many things have been told about this princess, so let's try and see what's REALLY TRUE and what's not:

SHE WAS THE DAUGHTER OF A RESPECTFUL NATIVE AMERICAN CHIEF. **TRUE!** Therefore, it is correct to call her a princess, as her father was like a king for his people.

SHE WAS IN LOVE WITH JOHN SMITH. **MAYBE!** We'll never know for sure, but we can be certain she almost lost her head for him.

HER NAME WAS POCAHONTAS. **FALSE!** That was her nickname as a child. Her real name was Matoaka, which means "she who loves playing."

**SPIRIT ANIMAL**

Witches, dark magic, dangers... princesses must face endless CHALLENGES before they can have their HAPPY ENDING! Having someone by their side is always a great idea. Unfortunately, not all of them can count on magical helpers like fairy godmothers or strong wizards. If you feel ready to become a "NATIVE PRINCESS" like Pocahontas, I suggest you choose a "SPIRIT" ANIMAL, an entity that embodies some specific qualities.

Hers was the **HORSE**, which represents freedom, but here's a short list of animals you can choose from:

the **DOG**: a faithful LOVE and FRIENDSHIP that never dies;

the **OWL**: the CLEVERNESS that allows you to find your way when everything seems dark;

the **COYOTE**: the CHAOS that shuffles elements together, creating new ones;

the **PUMA**: its STRENGTH and DETERMINATION help us face all sorts of challenges.

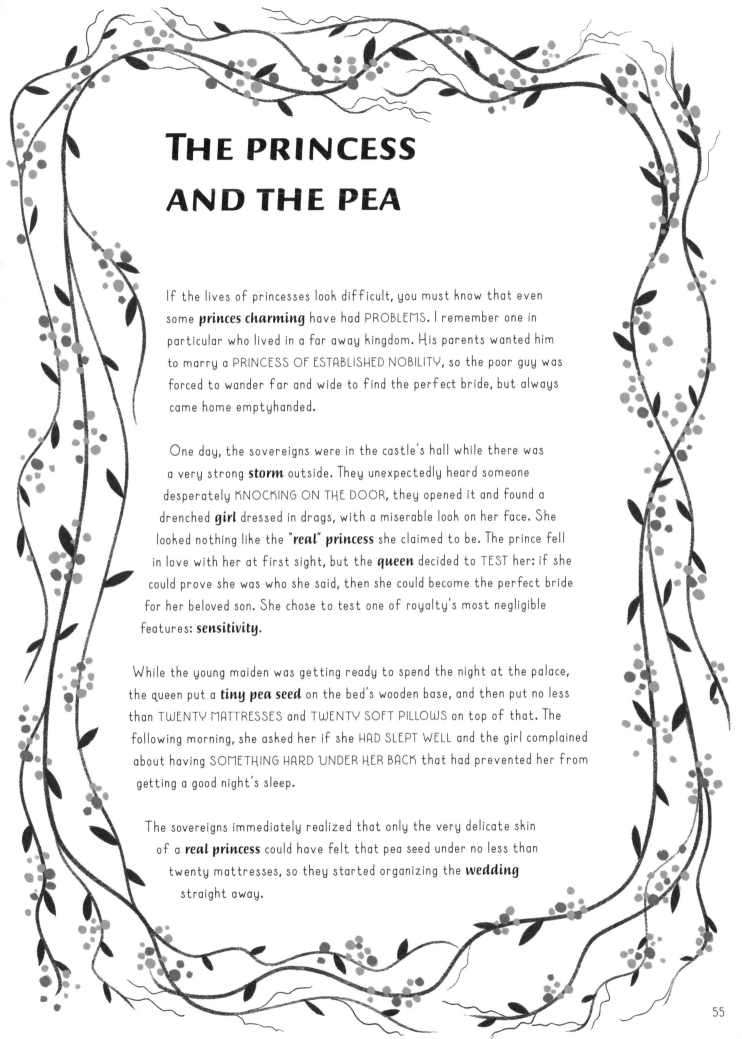

# THE PRINCESS AND THE PEA

If the lives of princesses look difficult, you must know that even some **princes charming** have had PROBLEMS. I remember one in particular who lived in a far away kingdom. His parents wanted him to marry a PRINCESS OF ESTABLISHED NOBILITY, so the poor guy was forced to wander far and wide to find the perfect bride, but always came home emptyhanded.

One day, the sovereigns were in the castle's hall while there was a very strong **storm** outside. They unexpectedly heard someone desperately KNOCKING ON THE DOOR, they opened it and found a drenched **girl** dressed in drags, with a miserable look on her face. She looked nothing like the **"real" princess** she claimed to be. The prince fell in love with her at first sight, but the **queen** decided to TEST her: if she could prove she was who she said, then she could become the perfect bride for her beloved son. She chose to test one of royalty's most negligible features: **sensitivity.**

While the young maiden was getting ready to spend the night at the palace, the queen put a **tiny pea seed** on the bed's wooden base, and then put no less than TWENTY MATTRESSES and TWENTY SOFT PILLOWS on top of that. The following morning, she asked her if she HAD SLEPT WELL and the girl complained about having SOMETHING HARD UNDER HER BACK that had prevented her from getting a good night's sleep.

The sovereigns immediately realized that only the very delicate skin of a **real princess** could have felt that pea seed under no less than twenty mattresses, so they started organizing the **wedding** straight away.

## AND THEY SLEPT, IN ANY CASE, HAPPILY EVER AFTER!

As a fairy godmother, it's hard for me to explain what features a royal bed
should have to guarantee princess-worthy dreams:
I've seen princesses curl up on dwarf beds and others nestled in a huge
oyster shell. POOR BRIAR ROSE LAY ON THE FLOOR FOR A CENTURY!
Therefore, you can choose the bed you want, but make sure you
have A FLOCK OF BIRDS TO WAKE YOU UP IN THE MORNING:
there's nothing better than STARTING YOUR DAY WITH
THE RIGHT SPIRIT!

## FUSSY, BUT NOT TOO MUCH!

She might be a "real princess," but allow me to say the protagonist of this fairy tale is too prissy and delicate!
IF YOU DON' WANT TO BECOME LIKE HER, here are two things you can do from time to time:

DON'T BE AFRAID OF GETTING DIRTY! Wear a pair of strong gloves and try to grow some flowers or maybe even a pumpkin: many princesses find it very useful;

DON'T BE AFRAID OF BEING UNCOMFORTABLE! To get used to it you should try sleeping in an enchanted forest: you'll find pebbles and twigs under your sleeping bag, but you'll have so much fun you'll barely even notice them!

## ANATOMY OF A "REAL PRINCESS"

ALL PRINCESSES ARE DIFFERENT, but over the years I've noticed they all have some features in common, ones the queen mother could have noticed even without troubling herself with stacking all those mattresses up!

1- "True princesses" NEVER GIVE UP, even after braving a storm and walking barefoot in the forest for hours.

2- They are always KIND, even when facing suspicious queens and uncomfortable beds.

3- They don't need to ask princes to prove their royalty: as long as he's Mr. Right!

# RAPUNZEL

Fruits and vegetables are good for you, we know that, but sometimes,
IF YOU ARE A PRINCESS, they are not a source of vitamins, they could actually
put you in trouble!
SNOW WHITE would have done much better without that APPLE, for example.

But no one had more trouble caused by a vegetable than **Rapunzel.**
Being born in a house overlooking a witch's vegetable patch is really a curse:
her mother was so PARTIAL to the **radishes** her daughter would then be named
after, she asked her husband TO STEAL THEM FROM THEIR NEIGHBOR.
But no one can escape the revenge of a **witch**! When Rapunzel is born the old
hag takes the baby and locks her up in a high, isolated **tower** without openings,
EXCEPT FOR A SMALL WINDOW AT THE TOP.
The girl is bored to death for years, her only diversion being braiding her
ever-growing **long blond hair,** and the witch soon uses it as a weird rope
to CLIMB THE TOWER.

This system, however, can't go unseen, and somebody is bound to notice the
two women sooner or later. RAPUNZEL GETS LUCKY: the first to discover this
peculiar elevator is a **prince.** Deciding to find out more, he climbs to the top of
the tower and ends up looking into the eyes of the girl of his dreams.

A HAPPY ENDING IS STILL FAR THOUGH!
The witch finds out about the meeting and, after cutting Rapunzel's ponytail
into a short bob, hides the girl in an **inaccessible cave,** casting a **curse** on the
prince to make him **blind.**
The young man, however, is not one who gives up and keeps on looking for his
beloved, until he finds her.
Rapunzel's tears of joy fall on the prince's eyes, he gets **his sight back** and can
see the girl's face again, framed by her new haircut.

## ANATOMY OF AN ENCHANTED TOWER

As it wasn't designed by an architect, but by a furious sorceress, it often leans on one side or the other, but never collapses because it's held together by MAGIC...

It's usually high, VERY HIGH ACTUALLY, to complicate the life of the young maidens locked up in there, and of the princes that fall in love with them.

## PRINCESS-LIKE HAIRSTYLES

Not all princesses have long blond hair, obviously. SNOW WHITE, for example, has always had short, coal-black hair. YOU CAN CHOOSE THE STYLE YOU PREFER: straight, curly, ginger, brown or even blue! But keep in mind that it would be really difficult to take care of your mane if it reaches 36 METERS OF LENGTH like Rapunzel's!

## WITCHES ARE REALLY TOUCHY!

There's the one who gets so offended she wasn't invited to
the christening of a baby princess she reacts by devising
a terrible deadly revenge; the one who dreams of
being a beauty queen and demands to have her
RIVAL's heart in exchange; and then there is this
LITTLE OLD LADY, who lOVES HER VEGETABLES
so much she takes her REVENGE on those
who stole one of her radishes by locking
an innocent girl in a tower.

SO ALWAYS REMEMBER THIS:
FAIRY TALE WITCHES ARE ALL
OVERSENSITIVE!

# THAKANE

I WANT TO DEBUNK A MYTH: princesses don't always put fashion first!
Thakane, the young and beautiful daughter of an **African chieftain**,
is surely not interested in it, unlike her two vain little brothers.
As they will soon attend a coming-of-age ceremony, the two princes need
clothes suitable to their rank, and it is **Thakane**'s task to find them.

IT SEEMS EASY, but the two boys won't settle for clothes made from the skin of
LIONS or CROCODILES. No, they even go as far afield as asking for **dragon skin**
clothes, something that you surely wouldn't find in the local market...

No one seems willing to follow Thakane in her difficult quest, except for **Masilo**,
the prince of a neighboring tribe. Together, the two cross Africa's planes, trying
to find an access in every pond, river or lake that might lead them to the underwater
world where the so-called **nanabolele**, aquatic dragons, live.
They finally arrive at the ancient village where the **old lady** taking care
of the DRAGONS lives.

Following her INSTRUCTIONS, the princess waits for the nanabolele to fall
asleep, then, with a swift attack, manages to creep up on them and kill
one, getting back to the village with her unhoped-for loot.

Her little brothers can finally get the clothes they wanted, while
Thakane has actually found something more precious than
fashionable clothes: the LOVE of a brave **prince.**

## ANATOMY OF A NANABOLELE

IT LOOKS LIKE A DRAGON: it's huge, has a long tail, serpent-like skin and all that, but it lives under deep AFRICAN RIVERS, emitting pale light in darkness; a feature that makes clothes made from its skin unique.

## OLD LADIES: YES OR NO?

After you read Thakane's story you might think that all old ladies in fairy tales are kind and eager to help. Unfortunately, this isn't always the case...
What does SNOW WHITE'S STEPMOTHER decide to transform into? AN OLD LADY! How old is the witch that keeps RAPUNZEL captive? VERY!
So, help is always welcomed, but before trusting someone you don't know, make sure her harmless looks aren't a disguise for BAD INTENTIONS.

## AN UNCOMMON PRINCE

Let's be honest, princes usually play hard to get... They take ages to arrive and reach the damsel imprisoned in a tower or under a wicked spell only when the story is almost at the end, just in time to get all the credit!

WELL, THE PRINCE THAKANE MEETS IS OF AN ENTIRELY DIFFERENT KIND.

First of all, he decides to help the princess because he was struck by her COURAGE more than by her looks.

Secondly, he follows her on her journey and NEVER LEAVES HER.

Finally, when he decides to marry her, IT'S ONLY FOR LOVE.

AN A-PLUS PRINCE!

# DULCINEA

Dulcinea is the princess whose story is linked to **knight-errant Don Quixote**, as she is always in his mind during his most heroic feats. Originally from Toboso, a village of **La Mancha** region, she is actually a girl of humble origins called **Aldonza Lorenzo**. Her beauty, grace, and kind heart make her so special in Don Quixote's eyes HE TRANSFORMS HER INTO PRINCESS DULCINEA.

Madly in love with her and determined to win her respect, Don Quixote asks to become a knight-errant and STARTS LOOKING FOR ADVENTURES. On the way, he meets **Sancho Panza**, a humble farmer who becomes his squire and CLOSE FRIEND. Together, the two comrades in arms take on eccentric but exciting feats, like BATTLING AGAINST WINDMILLS, puppets, flocks of sheep and every kind of characters. Every time, Don Quixote always thinks about the princess he left in La Mancha, singing the praises of her looks and moral qualities to his friend Sancho Panza.

He also WRITES PASSIONATE LETTERS to her, in order to reassure her of his noble intentions and to confirm that, faithful to his promise, he's doing everything he can to become worthy of her **love.** Their connection is eternal, WRITTEN IN THE STARS, something that doesn't break even with the death of the knight-errant who, until his last breath, has on his lips the name of his beloved princess of Toboso, the lovely **Dulcinea.**

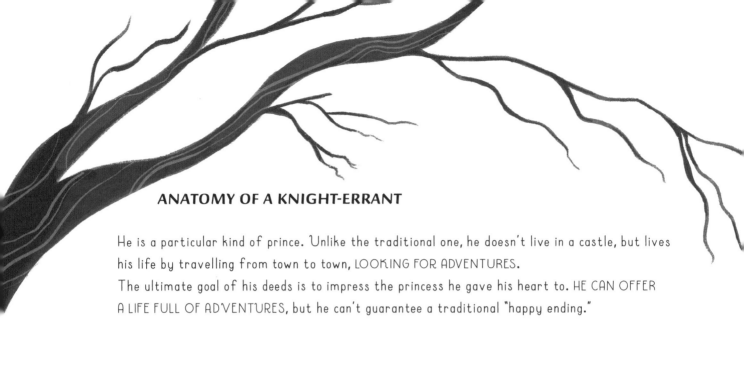

## ANATOMY OF A KNIGHT-ERRANT

He is a particular kind of prince. Unlike the traditional one, he doesn't live in a castle, but lives his life by travelling from town to town, LOOKING FOR ADVENTURES.
The ultimate goal of his deeds is to impress the princess he gave his heart to. HE CAN OFFER A LIFE FULL OF ADVENTURES, but he can't guarantee a traditional "happy ending."

## AN UNCOMMON MOUNT

Princes usually ride a steed: a pure-blooded horse with a nice stride and perfectly fit to take his knight into battle or to play a tournament. He must be striking to scare enemies off, and noble-looking to amaze a princess.

But not all knights and princes can afford horses that are so important... and EXPENSIVE!
Don Quixote, for example, must settle for the run-down ROCINANTE who is just a lousy work horse.
Even though he's old and skinny-boned, he proves himself to be at the same level as the best thoroughbred.

SO, HERE'S SOME ADVICE:
NEVER JUDGE A PRINCE BY HIS LOOKS, OR WHAT HE'S RIDING ON, BUT ALWAYS BY HIS HEART... AND BY HIS HORSE'S ONE!

## PEASANT VS PRINCESS

IT IS SAID THAT BEAUTY LIES IN THE HEART OF THE BEHOLDER. This is why, depending on who looks at her, the opinions about Dulcinea are so varied. If you happened to speak with Don Quixote, the man who is deeply in love with her, he would say:

**1-** She deserves to be crowned QUEEN OF THE UNIVERSE.

**2-** She's the FLOWER of all beauties.

**3-** She's a very WISE lady.

**4-** SHE'S THE WOMAN FOR WHOM I'LL BE GRATEFUL EVERY DAY.

If, however, you asked SANCHO PANZA, fateful confidant of the knight-errant, you would hear less flattering words, which are not polite enough to repeat in this book.

SO REMEMBER THAT YOU SHOULDN'T ALWAYS BELIEVE EVERYTHING THEY TELL YOU, AND AVOID GOSSIPING AS MUCH AS POSSIBLE!

## THE LOOKS OF A PRINCESS

HOW DOES BEAUTIFUL DULCINEA LOOK LIKE?
This is how Don Quixote describes her:
- Gold, blond hair
- Long, curvy eyelashes
- Pink cheeks
- Lips as red as coral
- Pearly teeth
- Shiny eyes
- Hands so white they look like ivory

ARE YOU THINKING WHAT I'M THINKING? WELL, YES... PRINCESSES ARE ALL TERRIBLY CHARMING. BUT DON'T WORRY, YOU ALSO HAVE WHAT IT TAKES TO BECOME LIKE THEM!

# THE PRINCESS
# AND THE SWANS

Luckily there are times when princesses live in families that are examples of TRUE LOVE, like the one that bonds **Elisa**, the sweet protagonist of this **fairy tale**, with her **eleven brothers**. SO THERE AREN'T ONLY EVIL STEPMOTHERS OR DISTRACTED FATHERS! Even though there are actually both in this fairy tale...

BUT LET'S START FROM THE BEGINNING! After becoming a widower, a king is forced to marry the **daughter of a witch**. His new wife soon shows her TRUE PERSONALITY, which is obviously cruel and **evil**. The first thing she does is sending Elisa into a farmer's hut, then SHE TRANSFORMS ALL HER BROTHERS INTO **swans**. The princess immediately tries to find them and, when she does, she discovers that the **spell** can be broken if she manages to **sew eleven shirts** made of **nettle**, in complete **silence**.

The love she feels for her brothers is so strong that the princess immediately starts sewing the stinging plants together and goes on doing so without ever whispering a word and despite the pain, until a **king** who has fallen in love with her decides to take her to his castle and marry her. THIS IS WHEN YOU WOULD EXPECT A HAPPY ENDING, RIGHT? Well, not yet, because the **queen mother** accuses the princess of practicing **black magic** and has her sentenced to be BURNED at the stake.

Some sort of **miracle** happens though because, just before being executed as a witch, the girl manages to finish the shirts and throws them on the swans that came in to help her: the curse is thus broken and her brothers are TURNED BACK INTO HUMANS. As the spell has been broken, Elisa can finally **speak** and prove her mother in law wrong. When he hears her story, THE KING HUGS HER AND HER BROTHERS.

## ANIMAL TRANSFORMATIONS

Curses that involve change are called "TRANSFIGURATION SPELLS."
Whether they are caused by a potion or by MAGIC WORDS, their aim is not only
to transform their unfortunate VICTIM, usually into an animal, but also to neutralize
him or her: if you are a frog, a swan or a fish it's really difficult to defend yourself
against a witch or wizard.
Don't worry too much about it though...
THE CURSE CAN BE BROKEN 99.9% OF THE TIMES!

## A LOT OF RELATIVES, A LOT OF TROUBLE?

I won't deny it, the family matters of the protagonists of our fairy tales are
often COMPLICATED: all those evil stepmothers and hateful stepsisters could
make us think that being an only child would surely help our heroines. I told ELISA
the same, but she disagreed with all her heart: she would never have given up on
her brothers' love!
WELL, WE CAN SAY SHE LIVED UP TO HER WORDS.

## ANATOMY OF A WITCH-STEPMOTHER

Most witches are beautiful women or sorceresses so powerful they enchant themselves to seem so. They are surely cunning and capable of charming naive kings, and they inevitably try to get rid of their daughter!
HOW CAN WE RECOGNIZE THEM?

**1-** They tend to be "the fairest of them all," or at least they try.

**2-** They use magic to convince the king to finally propose to them.

**3-** They try to get rid of the young princess in every way.

### BLACK MAGIC

Just speaking about it is SCARY, isn't it? It involves all those magical acts that aim to damage another person. To defend yourself you can run away or use WHITE MAGIC which, as you can tell from its name, doesn't harm anybody.

It's a bit too long to explain here, but I can tell you that all you really need to learn it and use it is one thing: A BIG, GOOD HEART.

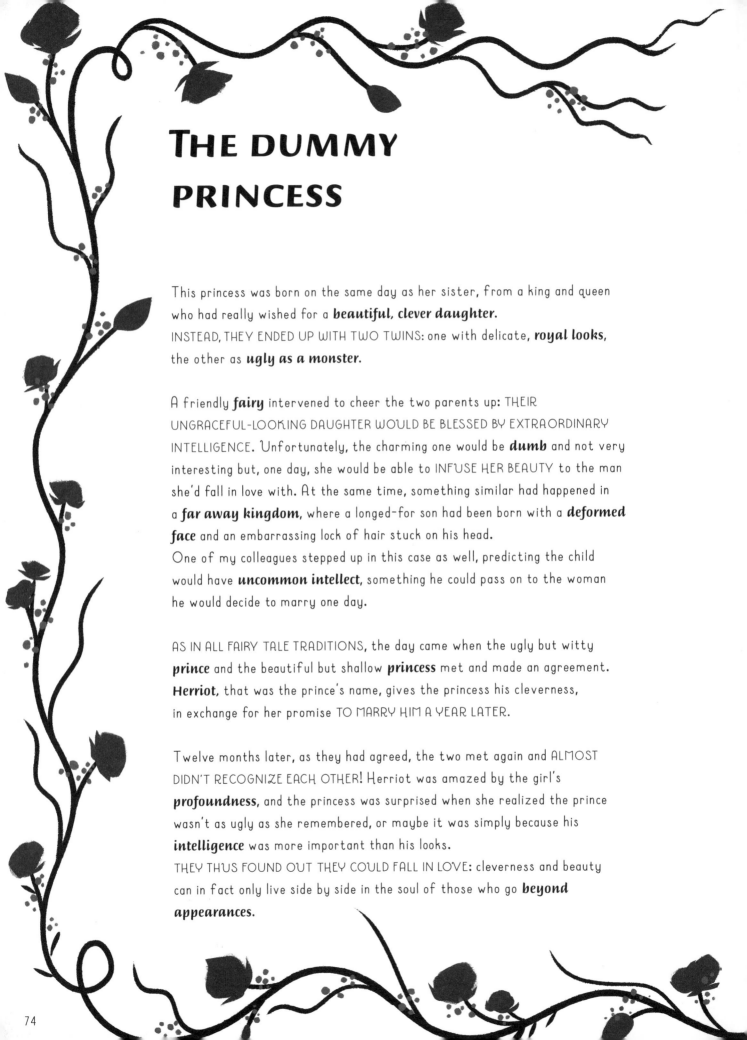

# THE DUMMY PRINCESS

This princess was born on the same day as her sister, from a king and queen who had really wished for a **beautiful, clever daughter**.
INSTEAD, THEY ENDED UP WITH TWO TWINS: one with delicate, **royal looks**, the other as **ugly as a monster**.

A friendly **fairy** intervened to cheer the two parents up: THEIR UNGRACEFUL-LOOKING DAUGHTER WOULD BE BLESSED BY EXTRAORDINARY INTELLIGENCE. Unfortunately, the charming one would be **dumb** and not very interesting but, one day, she would be able to INFUSE HER BEAUTY to the man she'd fall in love with. At the same time, something similar had happened in a **far away kingdom**, where a longed-for son had been born with a **deformed face** and an embarrassing lock of hair stuck on his head.
One of my colleagues stepped up in this case as well, predicting the child would have **uncommon intellect**, something he could pass on to the woman he would decide to marry one day.

AS IN ALL FAIRY TALE TRADITIONS, the day came when the ugly but witty **prince** and the beautiful but shallow **princess** met and made an agreement. **Herriot**, that was the prince's name, gives the princess his cleverness, in exchange for her promise TO MARRY HIM A YEAR LATER.

Twelve months later, as they had agreed, the two met again and ALMOST DIDN'T RECOGNIZE EACH OTHER! Herriot was amazed by the girl's **profoundness,** and the princess was surprised when she realized the prince wasn't as ugly as she remembered, or maybe it was simply because his **intelligence** was more important than his looks.
THEY THUS FOUND OUT THEY COULD FALL IN LOVE: cleverness and beauty can in fact only live side by side in the soul of those who go **beyond appearances.**

## 5 REASONS TO FAVOR A NERD

Surely not for his beauty, as he rarely has it, but for that rare kind of extravagant cleverness that charms you at first sight. WOULD YOU LIKE SOME EXAMPLES?

**1-** He knows all the NAMES OF CONSTELLATIONS and he'll probably find a NEW STAR while gazing at the sky and give it your name.

**2-** He'd be able to tell you about all the PROPERTIES PLANTS have, even the rarest ones, giving you precious insights on how to make creams and perfumes that no other princess knows about.

**3-** He can RHYME your name with the most beautiful words in most of the world's languages.

**4-** He can mentally do any COMPUTATION, even the most complex ones: it's extremely handy when you're ORGANIZING A PARTY with thousands of guests and you need to know how many plates you'll need.

**5-** He has EXCELLENT TASTE when it comes to combining shapes and colors and is thus super-duper useful when you are choosing what clothes to wear, for any occasion.

## INTELLIGENCE: A FAIRY'S GIFT?

It would be nice (and easy!)
but it doesn't work like that.
OK, you'll tell me, but Herriot's
fairy tale says that...
I'LL STOP YOU THERE: what it says
is that the prince's gift is being able
to instill wisdom in the ones he loves.
It wasn't enough for the princess to meet
him to improve her IQ, but that YEAR OF HARD
WORK was what she needed to understand that INNER
BEAUTY has more value than the external one.
SO, IF YOU WANT TO GET CLEVERER YOU NEED TO STUDY, A LOT,
AND SURROUND YOURSELF WITH CAPABLE PEOPLE WHO CAN
BROADEN YOUR MENTAL HORIZONS.

## ANATOMY OF AN UGLY PRINCE

Unlike other royal descendants, he's often terribly unattractive.
No one's head turns for him; actually, people usually look the other
way, poor thing! He's clever though, and has a virtue that's quite
rare nowadays: self-irony. He knows he's not handsome and
he's the first to laugh about it, playing it down.
He makes up for his uninviting looks by being a record-holder
chatterbox and telling hilarious jokes. You'll never get bored
with him and actually, after some time, he could even look
quite charming.

We are now, my dear, at THE END OF OUR JOURNEY.
You have listened to FASCINATING STORIES ABOUT MANY
PRINCESSES, some crafty and brave, others who are maybe
a bit too naive...

You have met CHARMING PRINCES, even though their looks
weren't always perfect, and you have learnt that THERE ARE
MANY KINDS OF ENEMIES that can make life seem far from
a fairy tale!
Well, you are finally ready!

All that's left is for me to give
you one last piece of advice:
make yourself comfortable on
YOUR THRONE and become
a truly unique princess.
Become YOURSELF!

# FEDERICA MAGRIN

Born in Varese in 1978, has worked in publishing for over ten years, first as editor of Edizioni De Agostini and now as a freelance. She mainly works in children's books, but also writes educational texts and stories and translates novels. In the past years, she has realized several books for White Star Kids.

# LAURA BRENLLA

Started learning to draw at the age of 16, but she grew up holding a pencil. She won a scolarship to study Art at Universidad Europea in Madrid, and once she graduated she specialized in cartoons in a two years course.
Later she was selected to receive a digital clean-up training at prestigious animation studio SPA, with Fernando Moro in charge. Strong drawing skills were developed. In the last few years she has illustrated several books for White Star Kids.

Graphic Design
**VALENTINA FIGUS**

White Star Kids® is a registered trademark property of White Star s.r.l.

© 2019, 2020 White Star s.r.l.
Piazzale Luigi Cadorna, 6
20123 Milan, Italy
www.whitestar.it

Translation: Langue & Parole, Milan, Italy

Revised edition

ISBN 978-88-544-1668-0
1 2 3 4 5 6   24 23 22 21 20

Printed in Croatia